Here is Miss Honey, the teacher
at Busytown School.
Color the picture.

Huckle is going to school today. Tell what is happening in each picture.

Where is Squeaky sitting? Draw a line connecting the dots and you will see. Then color the picture.

Draw a line under the things you can eat.

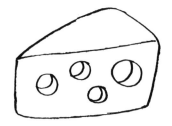

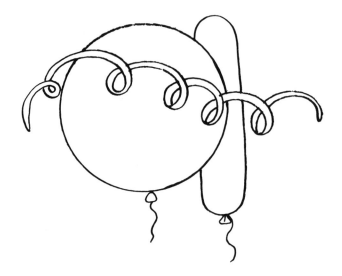

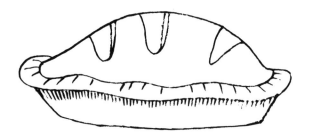

Huckle is playing ball during recess. Can you see where his ball lands? Help Huckle find it. Draw a line along the path to the ball.

Bruno is showing you how to draw an X.
Trace an X for each child below. Start at the dot.

Here are some more X's to trace. Start at the dot.

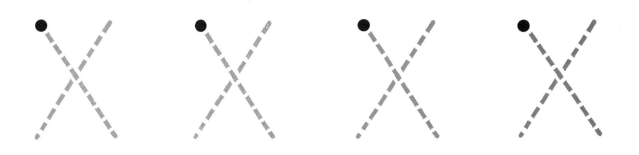

Look at the picture in each box.
Draw an X on the one who is doing the same thing.

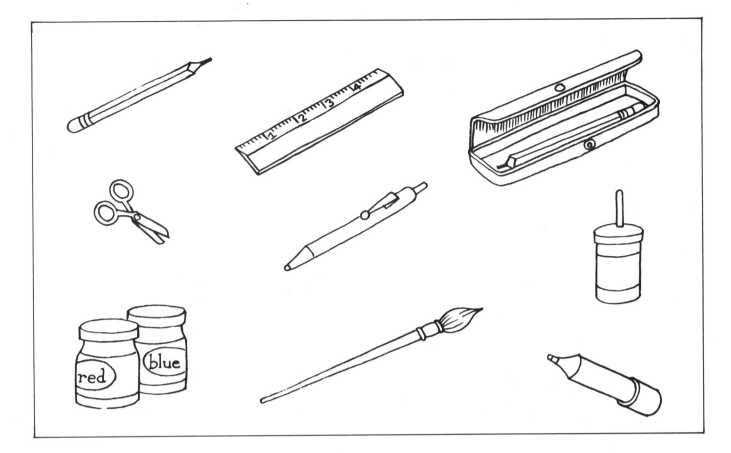

Mother Cat is shopping for school supplies for Huckle.
She wants to buy the ones on the checkout counter.
Draw an X on the same supplies in the box.
Can you name all the supplies you see there?

Draw an X on the one that is different in each row.

Very good, Huckle!

square

bell

star

diamond

triangle

circle

Huckle is drawing shapes
for Miss Honey. Can you name them?
Trace the shapes below and color them.

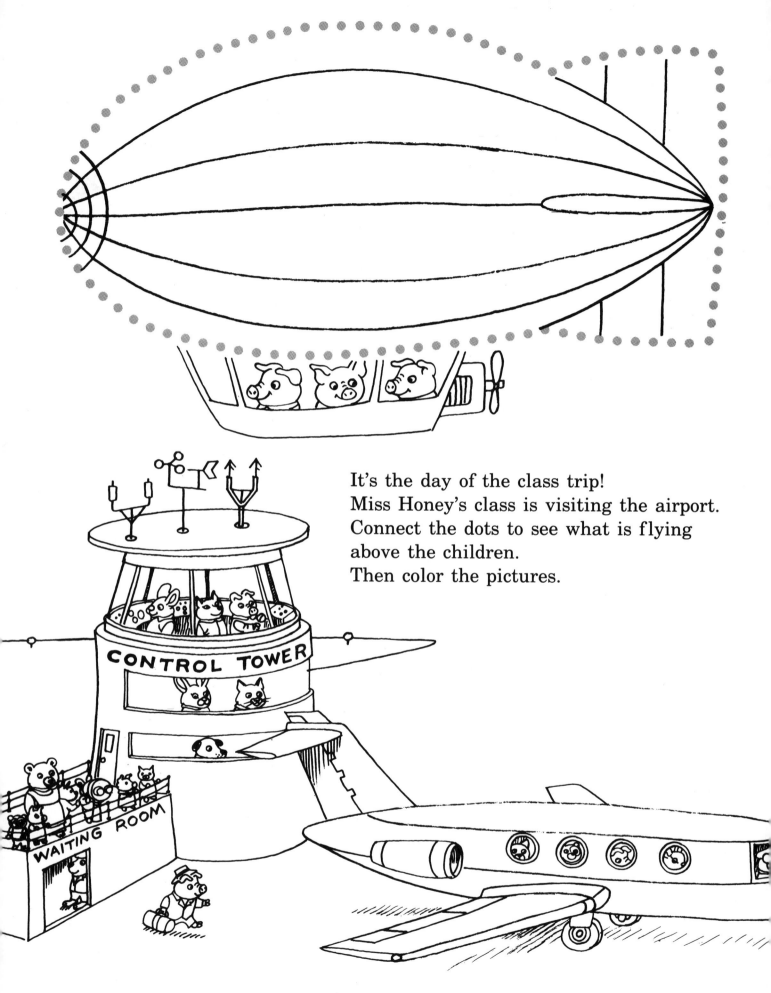

It's the day of the class trip!
Miss Honey's class is visiting the airport.
Connect the dots to see what is flying
above the children.
Then color the pictures.

CONTROL TOWER

WAITING ROOM

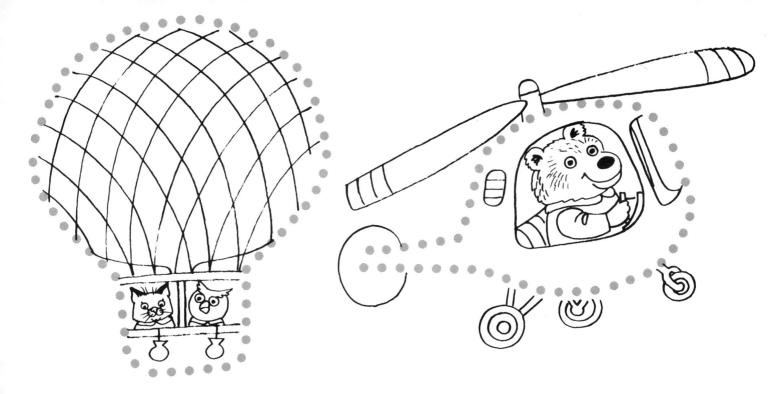

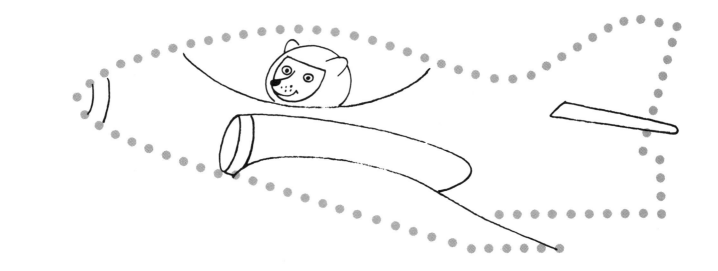

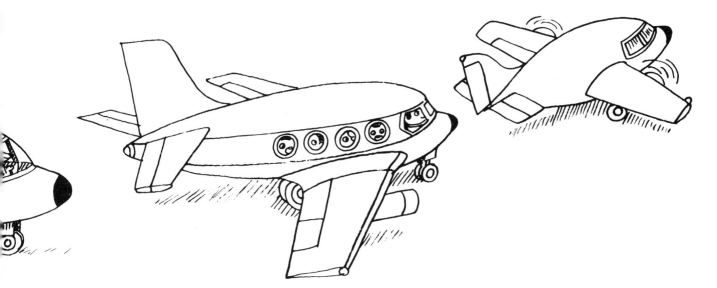

13

Draw a line from each thing to the picture where it belongs.

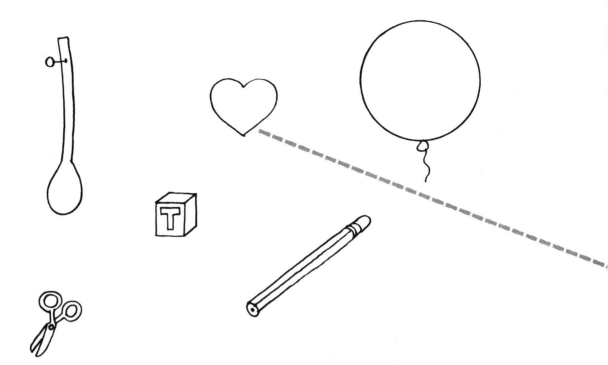

The children are on their way to school.
Connect the dots and you will see the school bus.
Then color the picture.

SCHOOL

Draw an X on the children who are outdoors.

Time for Show and Tell!
Huckle is telling the class
about his sea shell.

I found it at the beach!

Look at the things below.
Which one would you like to tell about?

Draw a line under the children who are indoors.

Miss Honey asks the children to draw a picture.
Look at the things below.
Draw an X on the ones the children can use to make a picture.

Aa *Aa* | Bb *Bb* | Cc *Cc* | Dd *Dd*

Draw a line from each thing at the bottom of the page to the one in the classroom that is the same.

SEPTEMBER

SUN	MON	TUES	WED	THU	FRI	SAT
			1	2	3	4	5
6	7	8	9	10	11	12
13	14	15	16	17	18	19
20	21	22	23	24	25	26
27	28	29	30			

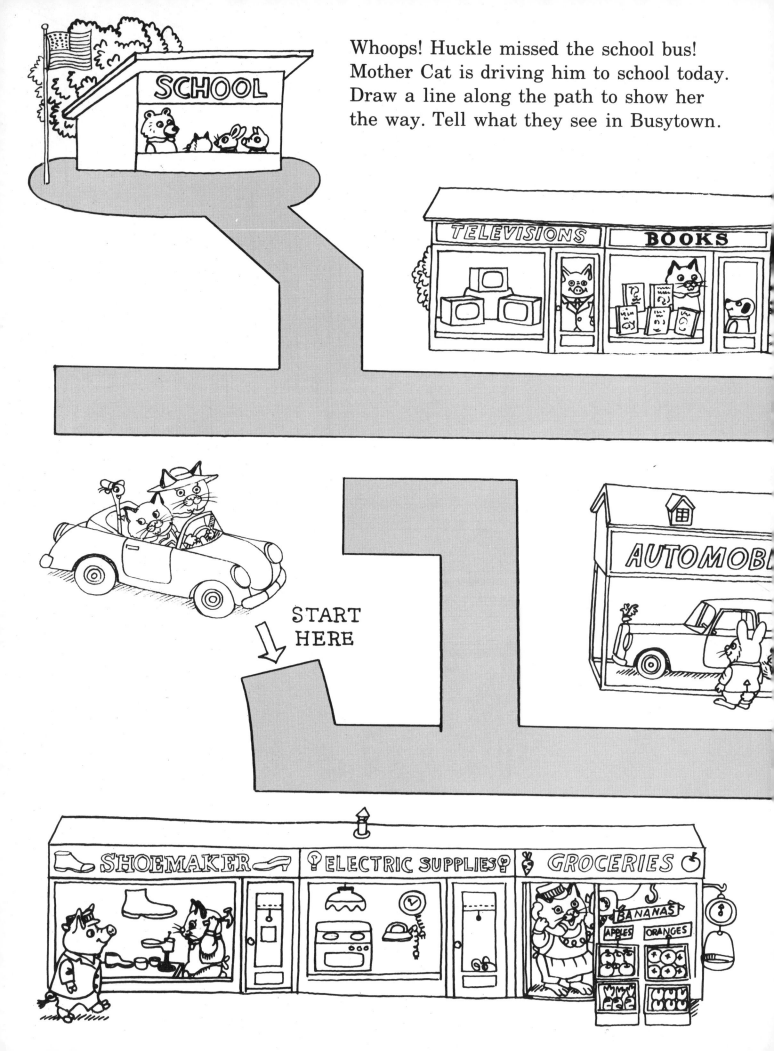

Whoops! Huckle missed the school bus!
Mother Cat is driving him to school today.
Draw a line along the path to show her
the way. Tell what they see in Busytown.

SCHOOL

TELEVISIONS BOOKS

AUTOMOB

START HERE

SHOEMAKER ELECTRIC SUPPLIES GROCERIES

BANANAS
APPLES ORANGES

Where did the shoppers come from?
In each row draw a line under the correct store.

Miss Honey has asked the children a question.
"Raise your hand if you know the answer," says Miss Honey.
Draw an X on each child who knows the answer.

Bruno brought home a good report card.
Connect the dots to see who is admiring it.
Then color the picture.

It snowed hard last night. School is closed today.
Draw an X on the things that the children would wear
to play in the snow.

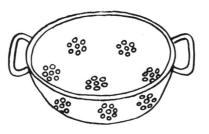

Huckle is going to skate around the pond.
Draw a line connecting the dots to see
where he goes.

Tell what Huckle sees
along the way.

Big Tilly loves small Lowly Worm! Color the picture.

The children are learning how to draw X's. You can too.

Trace the X's. Start at the dot. Then draw some more X's.

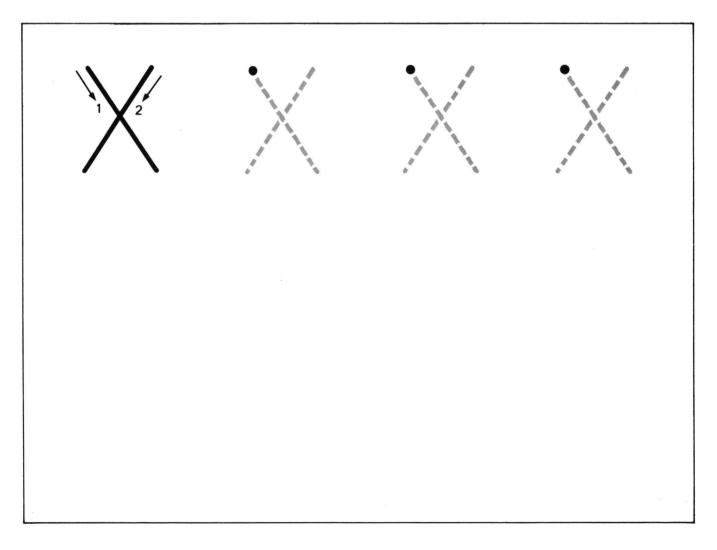

Huckle has something very big in his wagon. Draw a line connecting the dots and you will see what it is.

Now color the picture.

The wind is blowing!
The children can fly their kites today.
Some of the kites are big. Some are small.
Color the big kites.

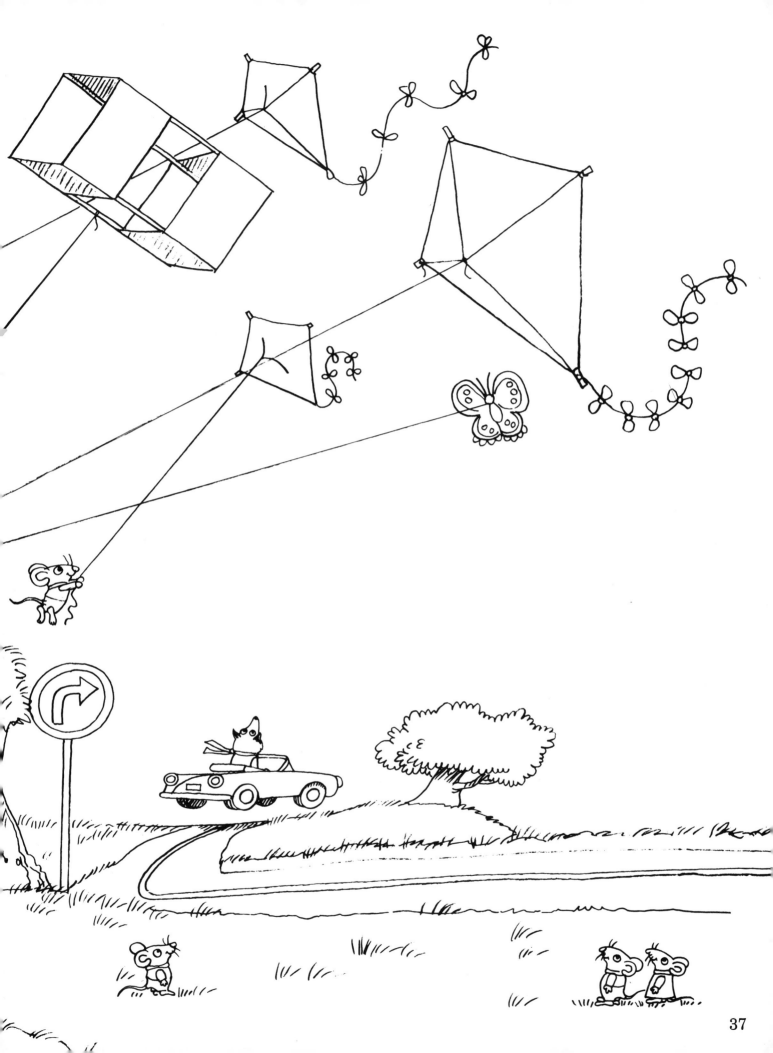

The mice have big balloons.
Bug has a bigger balloon.
Draw an X on the bigger balloon.

Draw an X on the bigger flower.

Draw an X on the child who is eating the bigger piece of watermelon.

38

Lowly and Tilly
each baked a cake.
Lowly's cake is smaller
than Tilly's cake.

Draw an X on the smaller toy.

Draw an X on the smaller house.

Draw a line under the one that is the same size as the one in the box.

Draw a line connecting the dots to see who is sitting in the small seat.

In each row draw an X on the one that is not the same size.

Huckle is taller than Lowly Worm.
Color the picture of the two friends.

Early Bird is shorter than Benjamin Rabbit.
Color the picture.

Color the one who is taller.

Color the one who is shorter.

The banana car is longer
than the pencil car.
Color the banana car.

Color the truck that is longer.

The sausage car is shorter than the pencil car.

Draw an X on the boat that is shorter.

Willy Pig is going for a walk on the beach.
Draw a line connecting the dots to see
his path. Tell what he sees along the way.
Draw an X on something big in the picture.
Draw a line under something small.

EAT BRUNO'S HOT DOGS

BRUNO'S HOT DOGS

LIFE GUARD

LIFE GUARD

Kitty has a small balloon.

Huckle has a big balloon.

big

bigger

Benny Baboon has
a bigger balloon.

biggest

Run!
It's going
to burst!

Polly Pig has the biggest balloon.
Watch out, Polly! Don't blow too hard!

Color the biggest balloon.

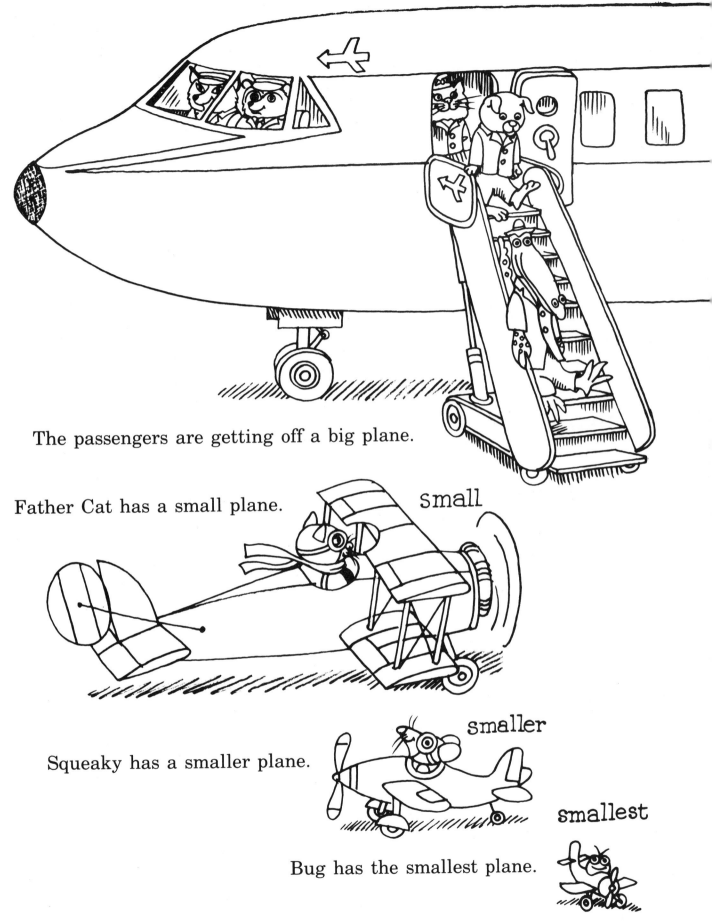

The passengers are getting off a big plane.

Father Cat has a small plane.

small

Squeaky has a smaller plane.

smaller

Bug has the smallest plane.

smallest

Draw an X on the smallest plane.

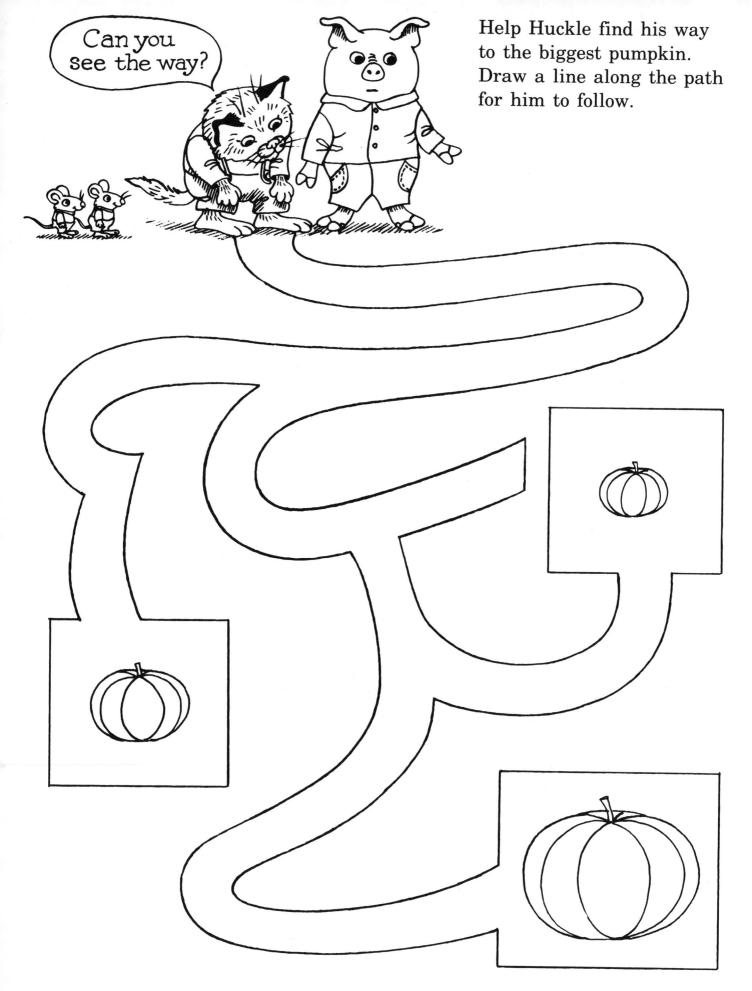

Draw a line under the tallest one in each row.

Draw an X on the shortest one in each row.

Draw a line connecting the numbers that are the same.

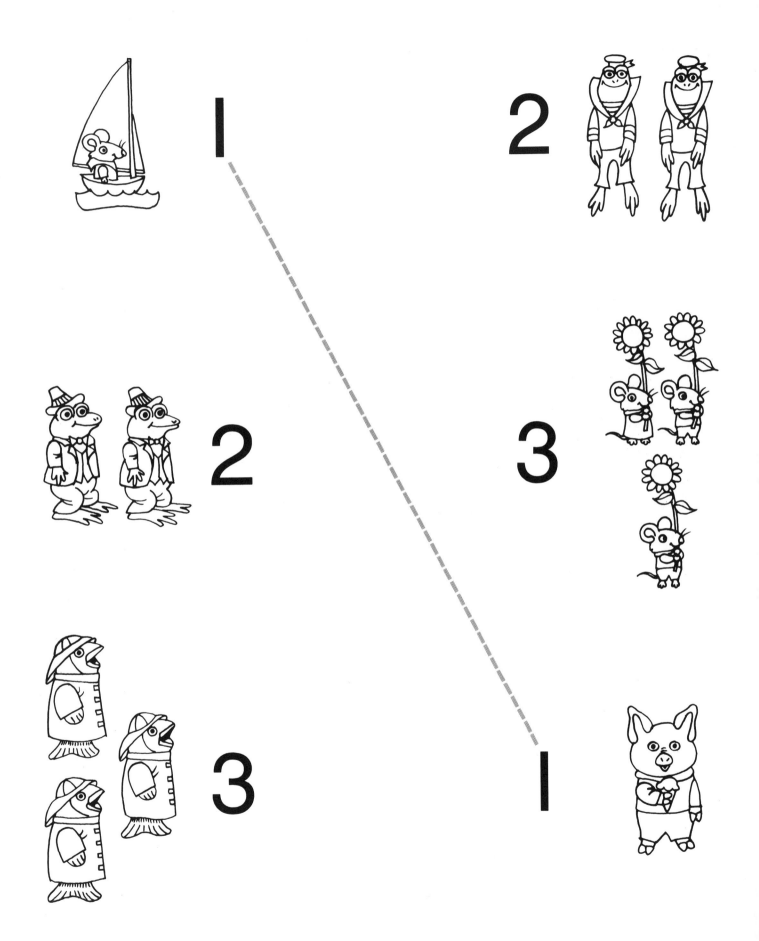

There's lots to see in Busytown's shops.
Draw a line from the things at the bottom of the page
to the same things in the shop windows.

These shops are on Busytown Street.
Which shop has the address 3 Busytown Street?

Draw a line connecting the numbers that are the same.

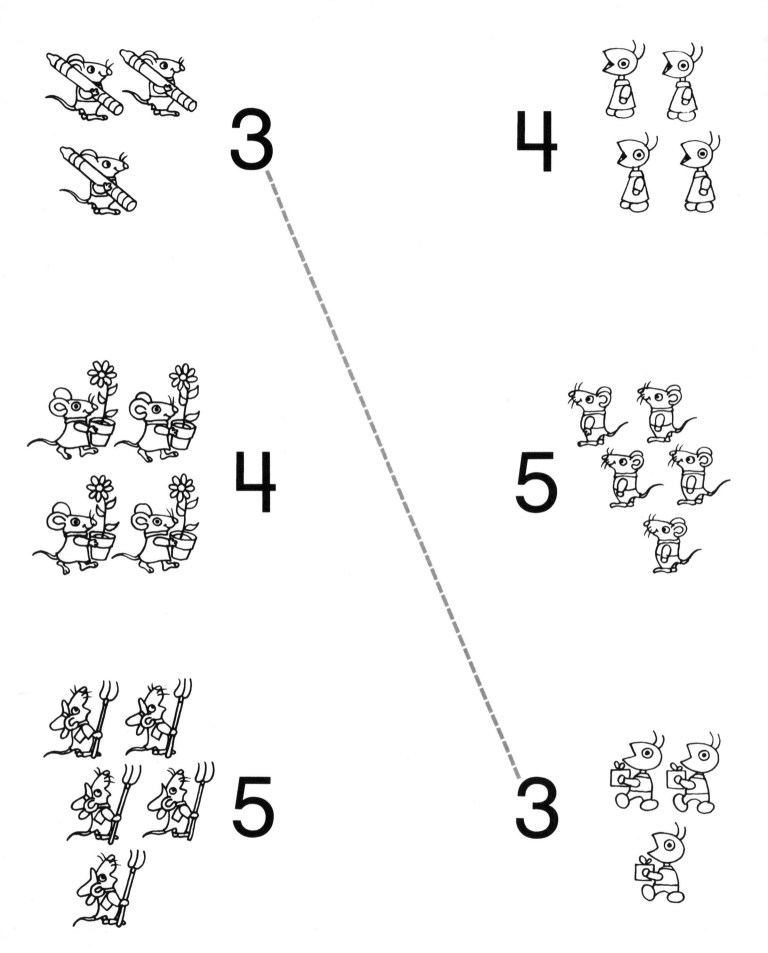

Draw a line from each number to the plane with the same number
and the child with the same number.

Draw a line connecting the same numbers.
Color the children who are holding the number 5.

Trace the numbers. Start at the dot.
Count how many friends are next to each number.

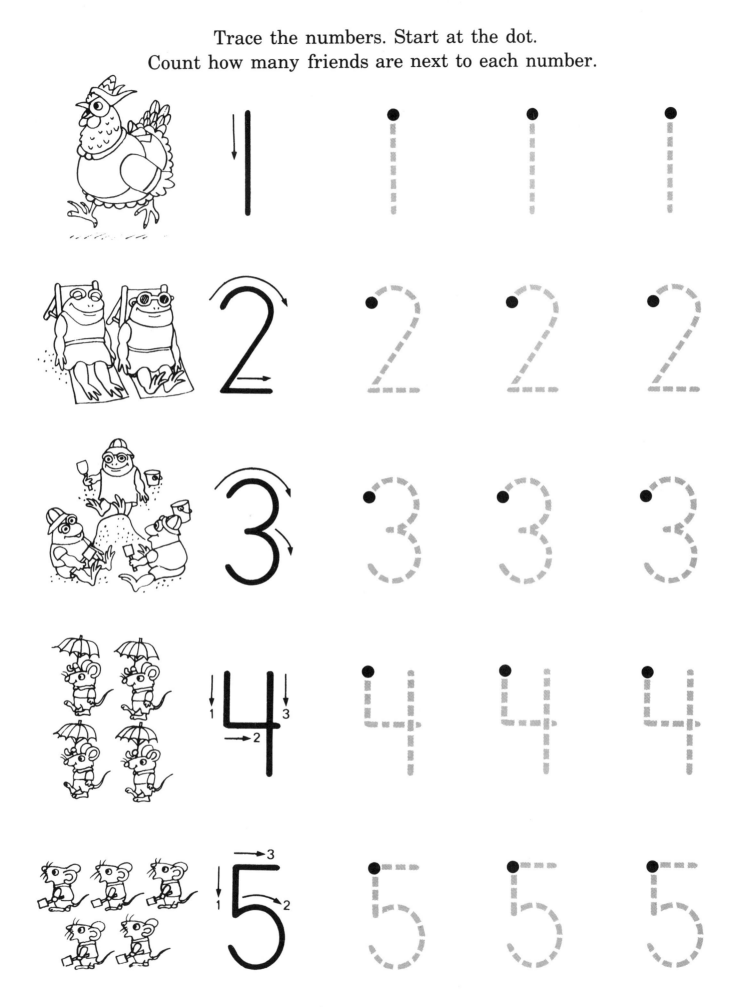

Ask a grownup to color the crayons.
Then help Becky Bunny find an apple.
Color each box with a 2 in it blue
and you will make a path to the apple.
Now find a carrot for Billy Bunny by
coloring each box with a 3 in it red.

I'd like a carrot!

BLUE 2   3 RED

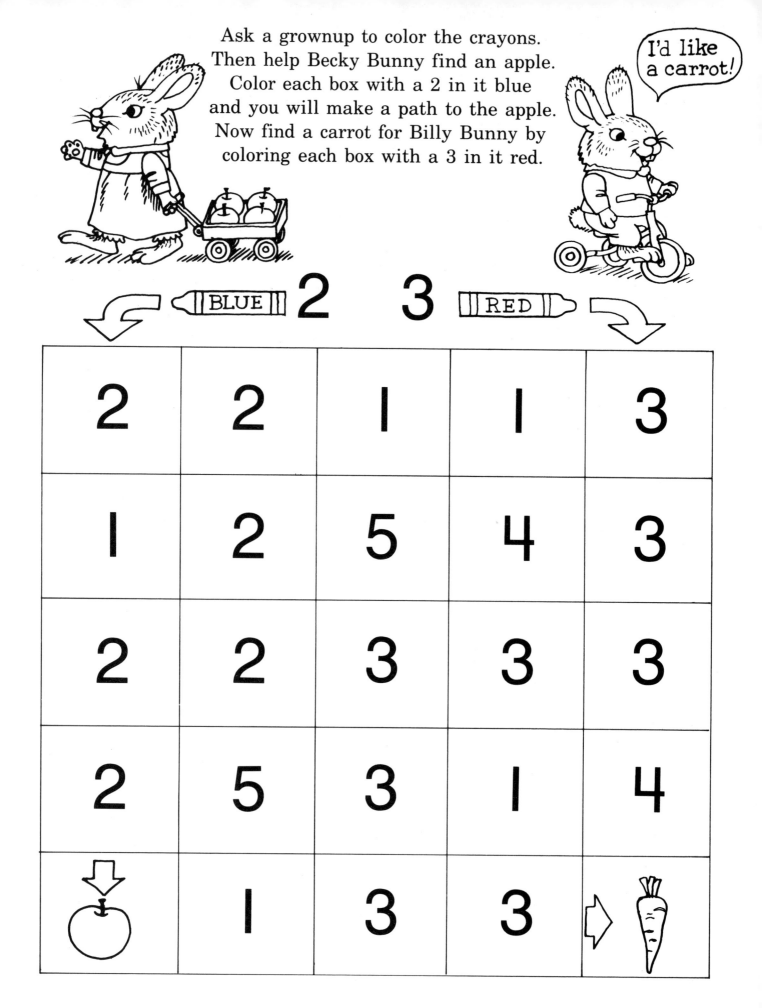

2	2	1	1	3
1	2	5	4	3
2	2	3	3	3
2	5	3	1	4
🍎	1	3	3	🥕

62

How many? Count the children next to each box.
Then trace the number in the box.

Draw a line connecting the dots in order – 1, 2, 3, 4, 5.
Then color the pictures.

START HERE

2

3

4

1

5

START HERE

2

1

3

5

4

64

Help Lowly Worm get up and go! Color his picture.

Sailor Mouse is going to sail through the harbor.
Draw a line connecting the dots to see where he goes.
Tell what he sees along the way.

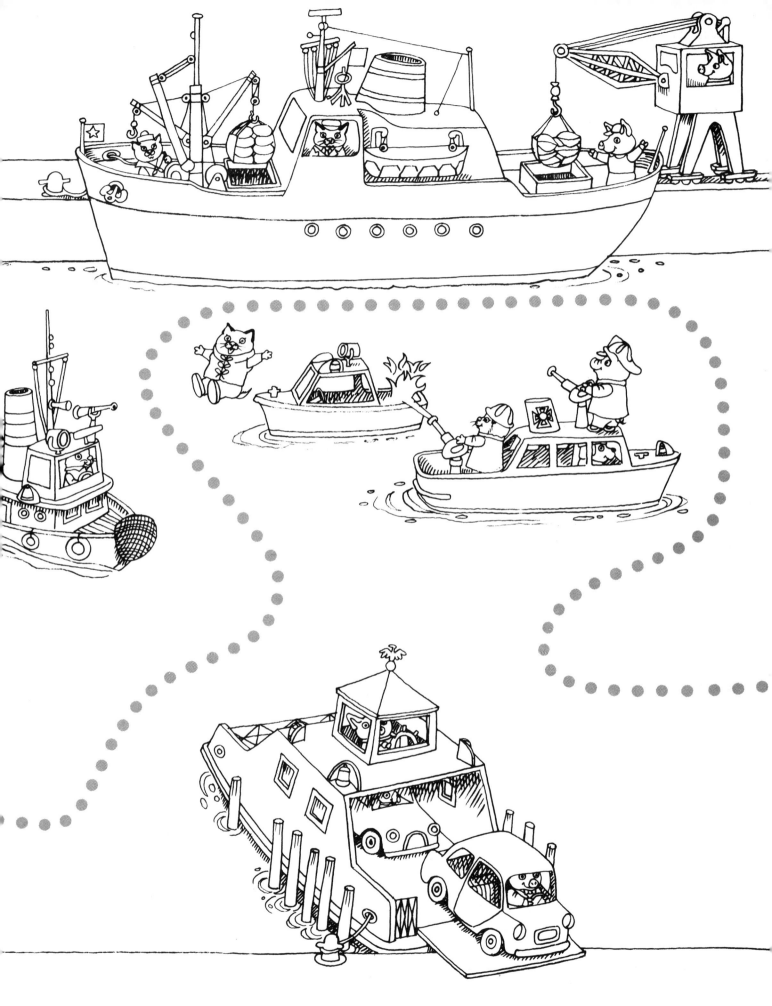

Huckle is showing you how to draw different kinds of lines.

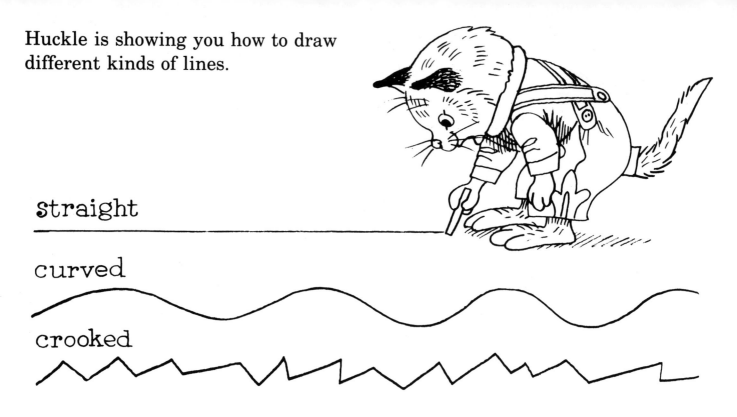

straight

curved

crooked

Draw a straight line, a curved line, and a crooked line.

Can you guess what I am doing?

Trace the two circles around the clock face.
Color the clock.

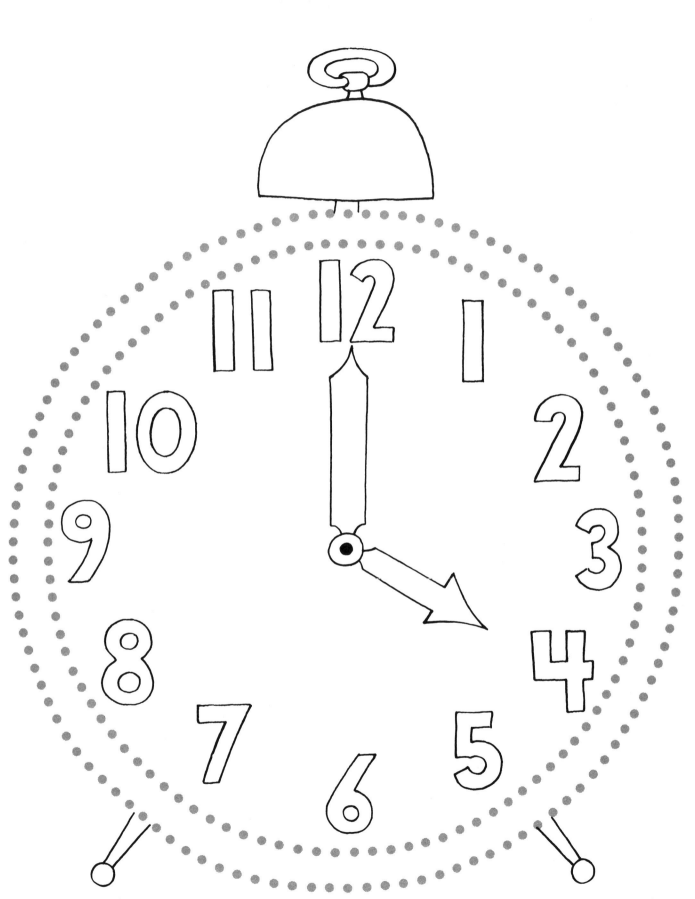

START HERE

Lowly is showing you how to draw a circle.

A balloon is round like a circle. Draw balloons for the mice. Start at the dot. Then color the balloons.

Brrr! It's cold on the skating pond.
Now the children want to go to Grandma's
house for hot chocolate. Draw a line along
the path for the children to follow.

This is fun!

Draw a flower for each pot.
The dots will show you how.
Then color the flowers.

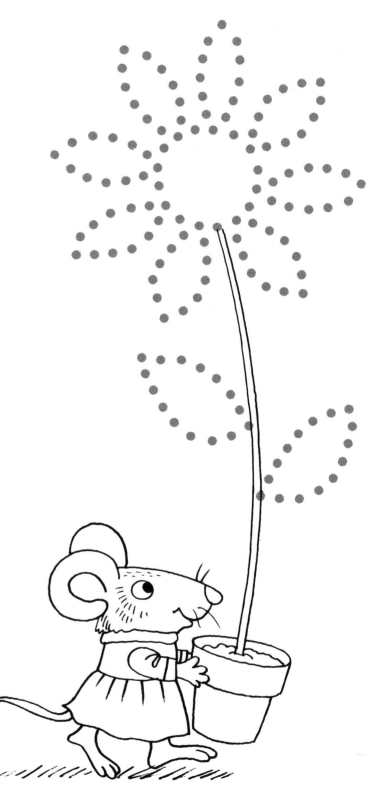

Connect the dots to see
what Miss Honey is playing.
Color the picture.

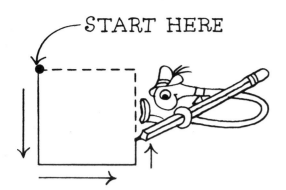

START HERE

Lowly is showing you how to draw a square.

Robert Rabbit is building a block tower.
The blocks are shaped like squares.
Trace the blocks. Start at the dot.
Then draw some more squares
for Robert's tower.

Timber-r-r!

Who is drawing a picture of Bug?
Connect the dots and find out.

Lowly is showing you how to draw a triangle.
Trace the other triangle. Start at the dot.

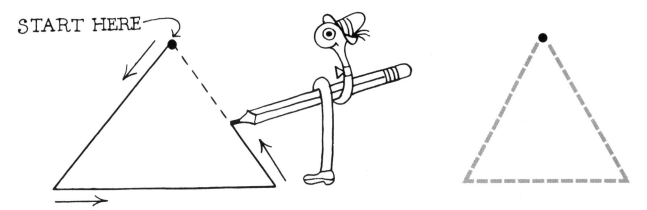

START HERE

Willy Pig has a hat and flag shaped like triangles.
Trace the hats and flags of the other children. Start at the dot.

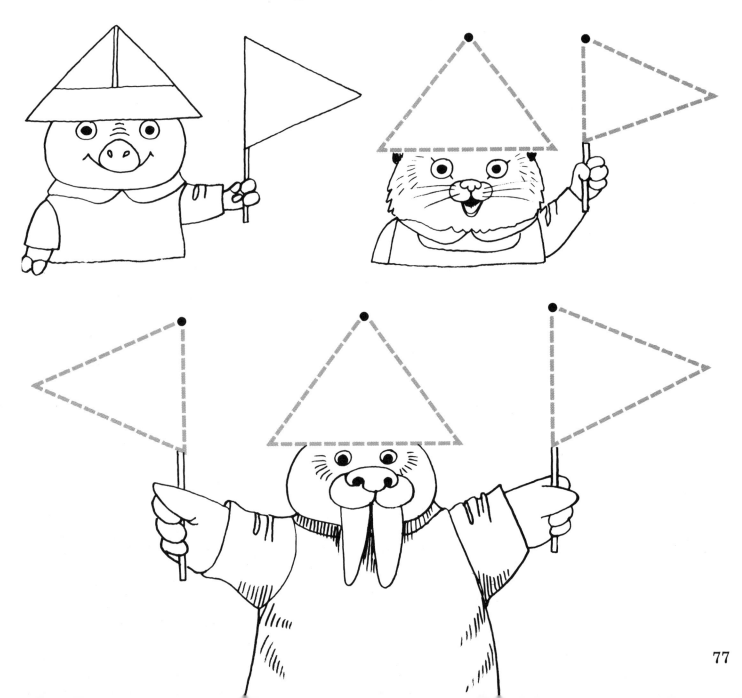

77

Lowly Worm loves apples. Help give him some more.
Draw a line connecting each set of dots. Color the picture.

Lowly is hungry! Draw some apples on his plate.
Then color the picture.

Oliver Octopus has lots of arms
for carrying things.
What would you like him to carry?
Look at the things above Oliver.
Draw one on each arm that is free.
Then color the picture.

Dr. Bones is giving Huckle a checkup.
Tell what is happening in each picture.

Trace the box around each picture.

Welcome to Busytown! Draw a line from each sign to the one in the picture that is the same.

84

Draw a picture of the thing that each child is holding.

Huckle wants to play outdoors in the cold.
Draw a hat and boots for him.

Tell what you can buy in these Busytown shops.
In each box draw something you would like to buy.

Trace the letters. Start at the dot.

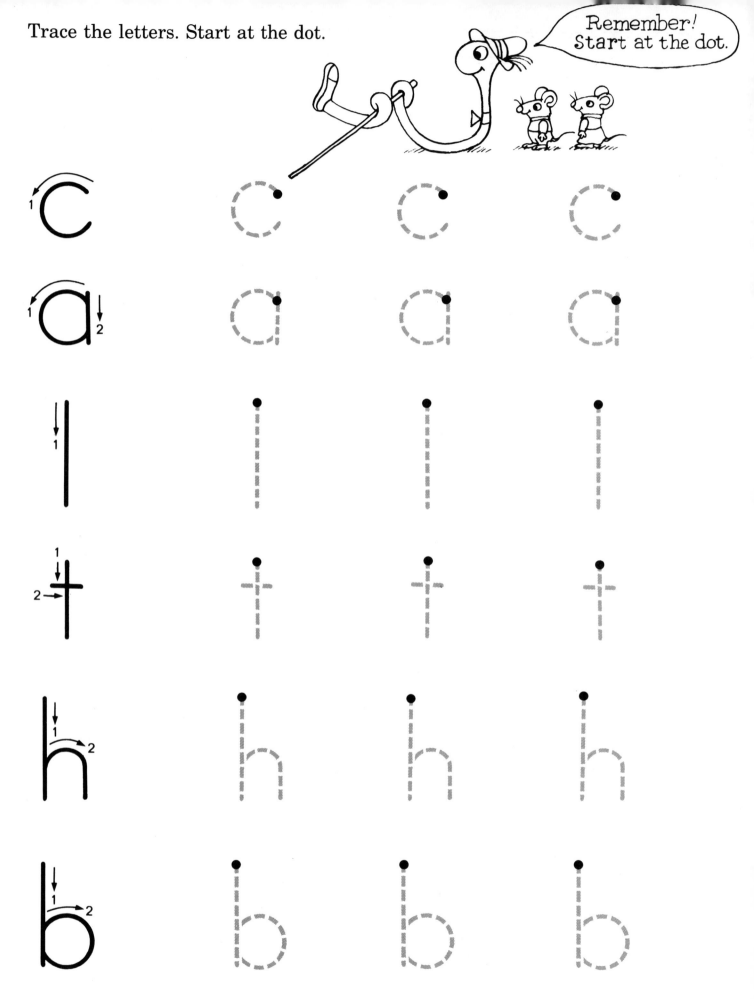

Remember!
Start at the dot.

Trace the letters of each word.
Start at the dot.

cat

hat

bat

ball

Trace the letters of each word. Start at the dot.

bat

hat

ball

cat

Roger Raccoon is drawing pictures of his friends.

Draw a picture of someone you like.

Look at the sign in the box.
Then draw a circle around the sign that is the same.

Trace the letters in each word. Start at the dot.

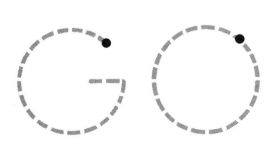

Help Huckle and Lowly write their names. Trace the letters.

Huckle

Lowly

Ask a grownup to write your name on the first line below.
Then you write your name on the second line.

Huckle and his friends are on their way
to the library. Color the picture.

Look at the child in the box. Draw a line under the child who is the same.

Time to go shopping!
What do Mother Rabbit and Ms. Mouse want to buy?
Draw a line connecting each set of dots and you will see.

Now color the pictures.

Draw a line connecting the ones that look the same.

**Tell about the games
the children are playing.
Which game do you like best?**

leapfrog

jump rope

marbles

tag

ring-around-the-rosy

hopscotch

1 2 3 4 5 6 7 8

Betsy Bear wrote a letter to Grandpa.
Now she wants to mail it.
Draw a line along the path
from Betsy's desk to the mailbox.

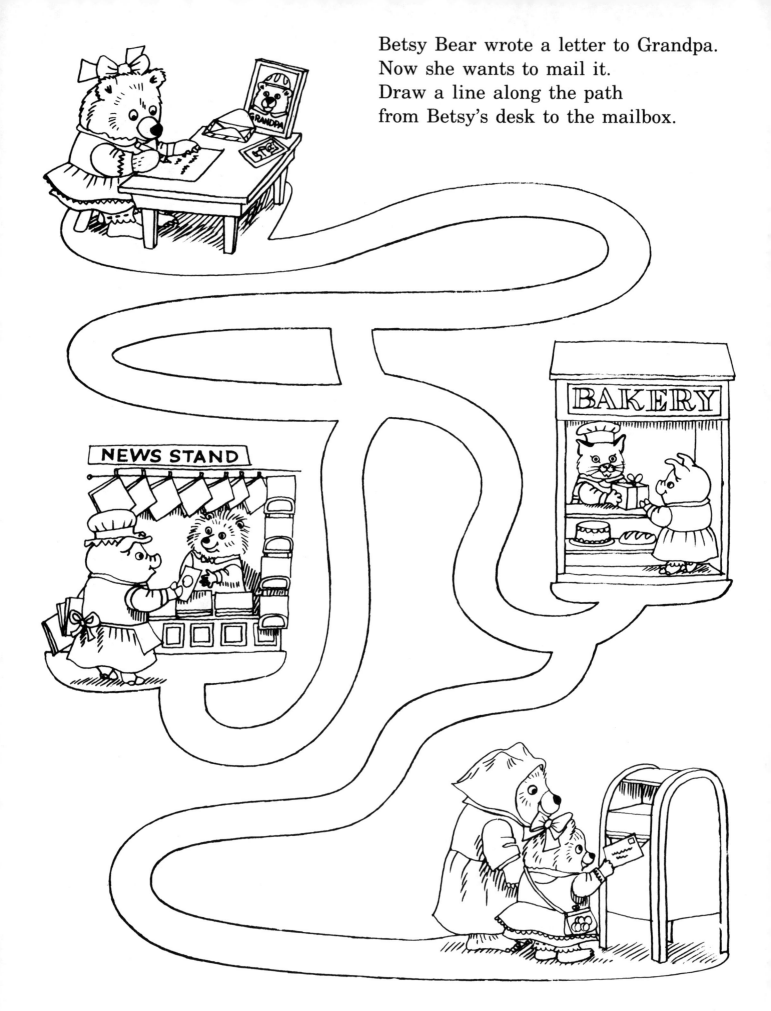

Draw a line under the ones that look the same.

Color the one that is different.

Polly Pig is making a necklace.
Uh-oh! She needs some help.
Will you draw some beads for
her necklace?

START HERE

A bead is round like
a circle. Here is a circle
for you to trace. Start
at the dot.

Ooops!

Trace these circles to give
Polly some beads.
Then color the necklace.

Polly will be so happy!

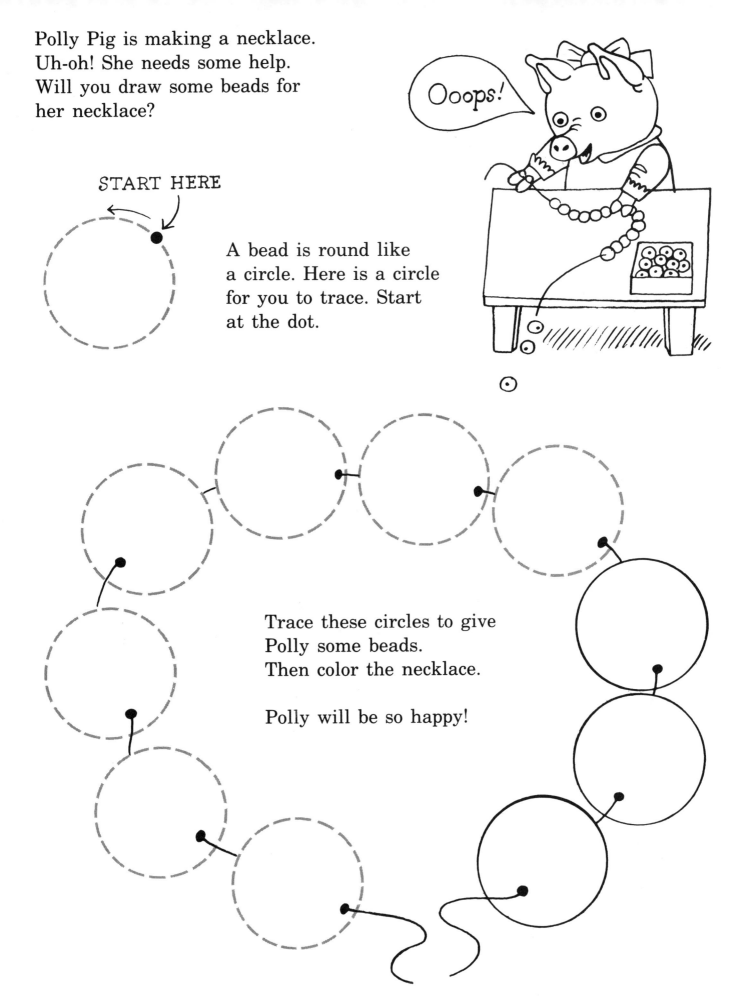

Draw a circle around the one that is different.

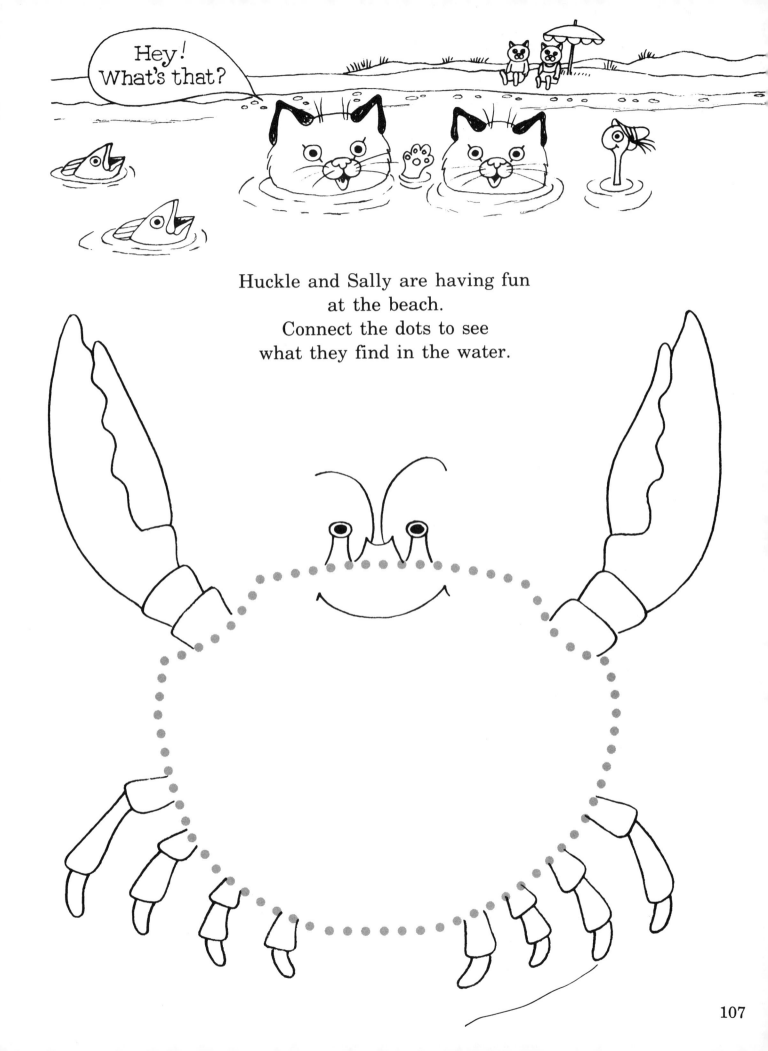

Huckle and Sally are having fun
at the beach.
Connect the dots to see
what they find in the water.

107

It is raining very hard,
but Huckle won't get wet.
Can you tell why?

Draw a circle around the things that will keep Huckle dry.

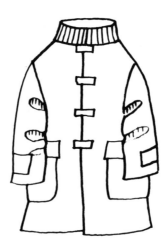

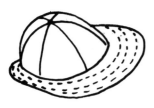

FRUITS

Sally is going to buy the fruit at the bottom of the page. Draw a line from each fruit to the one in the box that is the same.

Some grapes, please, and...

What tools are the workers using?
Draw a line from each worker to the correct tool.

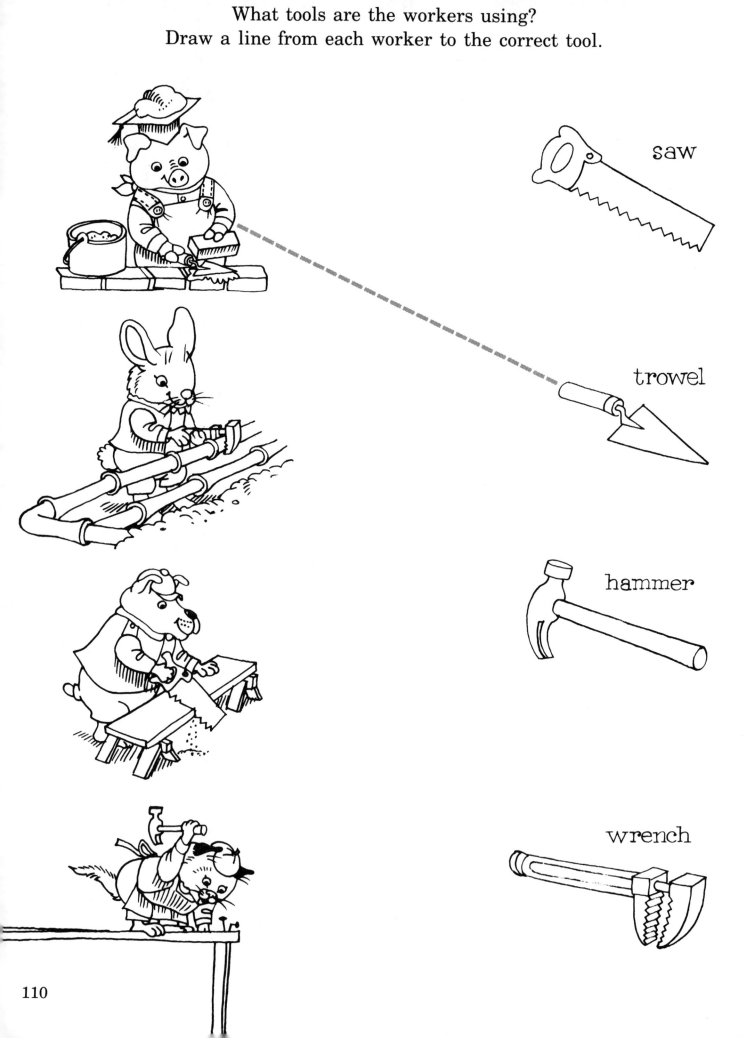

saw

trowel

hammer

wrench

VEGETABLES

The shoppers want to buy the vegetables
at the bottom of the page.
Draw a line from each vegetable to the one
in the box that is the same.

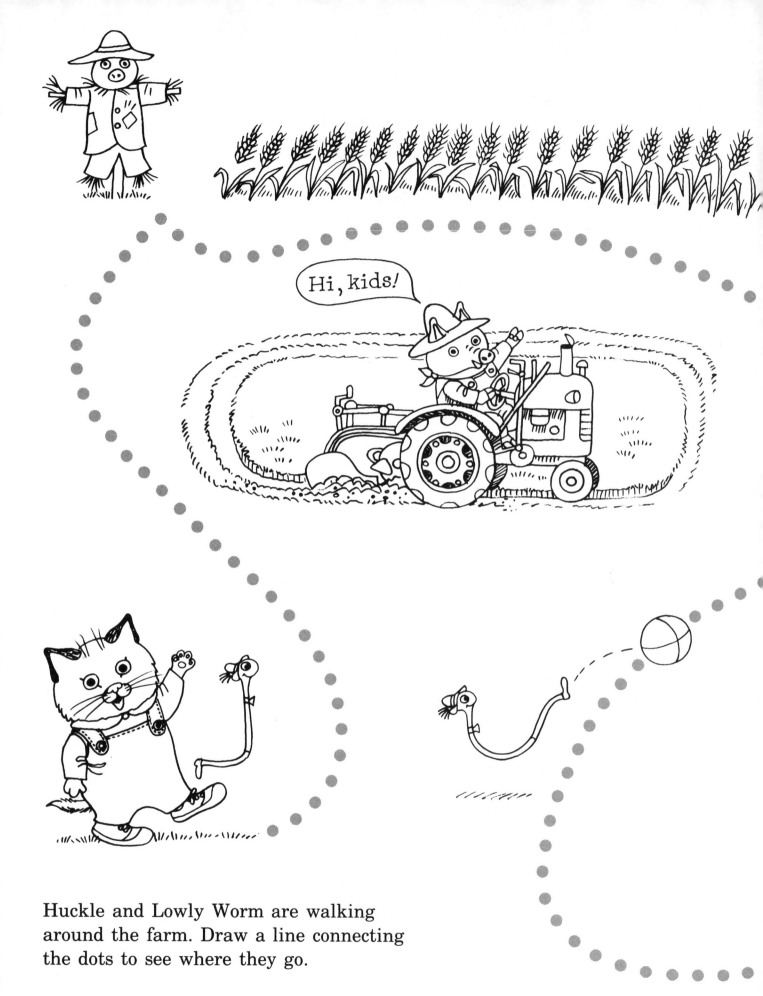

Hi, kids!

Huckle and Lowly Worm are walking
around the farm. Draw a line connecting
the dots to see where they go.

Tell about the things they see
along the way.

Picnic time! The children are eating hot dogs and ice cream.
Draw a line from the grill to each child who has a hot dog.
Draw a line from the ice cream buckets to each child who has an ice cream cone.

Oh, dear! Captain Tilly is in trouble!
Tell what is happening.

Draw a line connecting the things that go together.

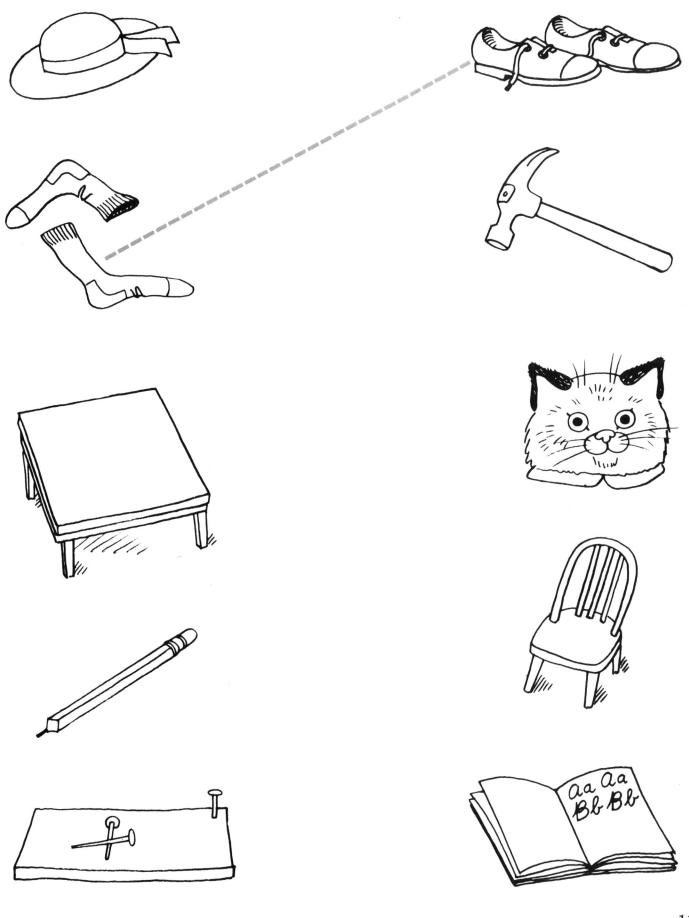

The pilot goes with the airplane.
Can you tell what the other people go with?
Draw a line from each person to the correct thing.

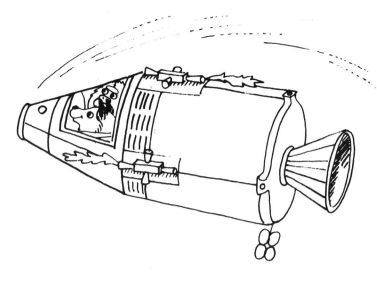

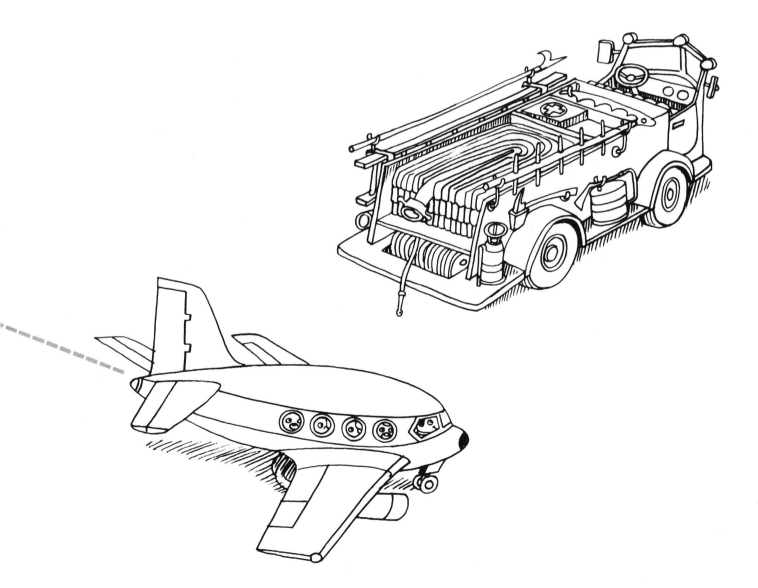

Look at the pattern in each row.
Draw a circle around the one in the box that continues the pattern.

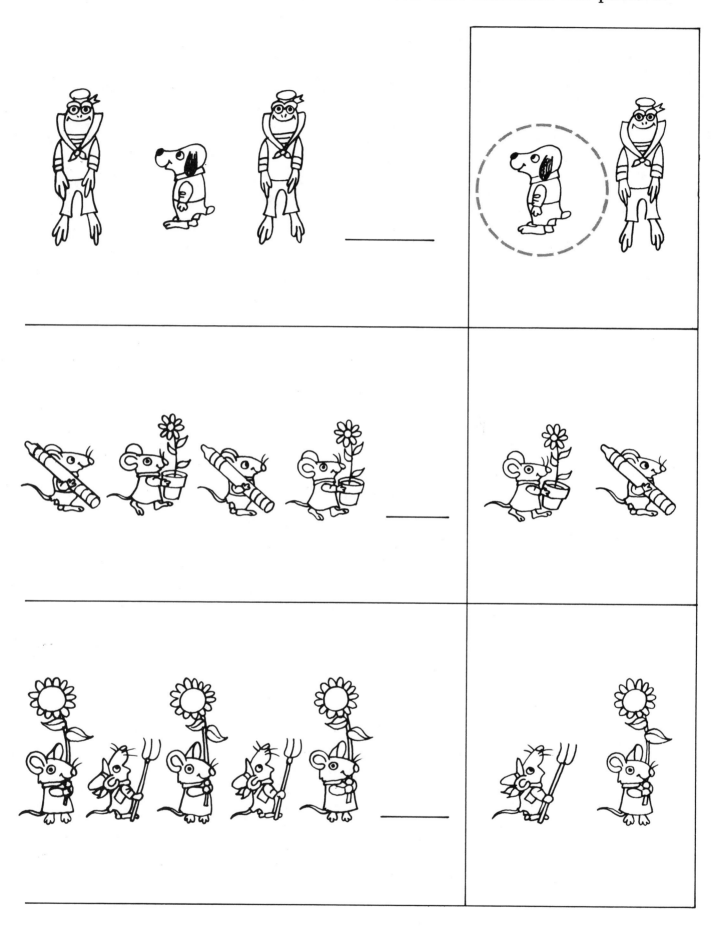

Lowly loves apples. Willy Pig loves ice cream. Flossie Bunny loves carrots. Draw a line along the path from each child to his or her favorite food.

YUM!

Look at the pattern in each row.
Draw a circle around the one in the box that continues the pattern.

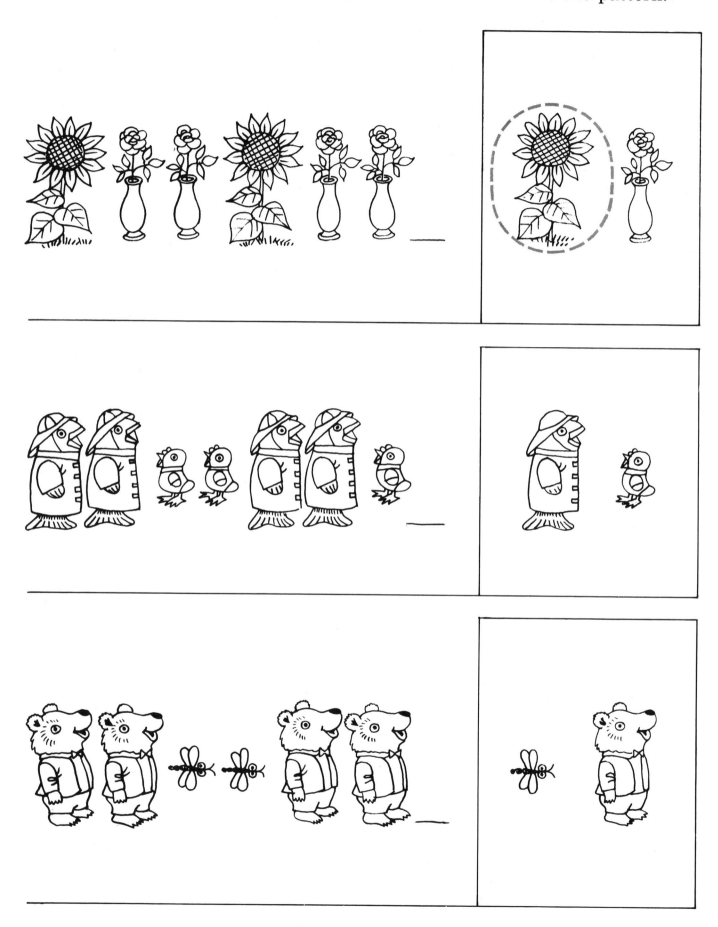

Look at the letter in each box.
Draw a circle around the letter that is the same.

Busytown is full of signs.
Draw a line from each sign at the bottom
to the one in the picture that is the same.

EAT BRUNO'S HOT DOGS

TOWN HALL

POST OFFICE

LIBRARY

EAT BRUNO'S HOT DOGS

Busytown is full of traffic!
Connect the dots to see
what is going by on the street.

Ask a grownup to color the crayons.

RED	Color the bus red.
YELLOW	Color the taxi yellow.
GREEN	Color the car green.
BLUE	Color the truck blue.

Draw a line connecting the balloons with the same letter.

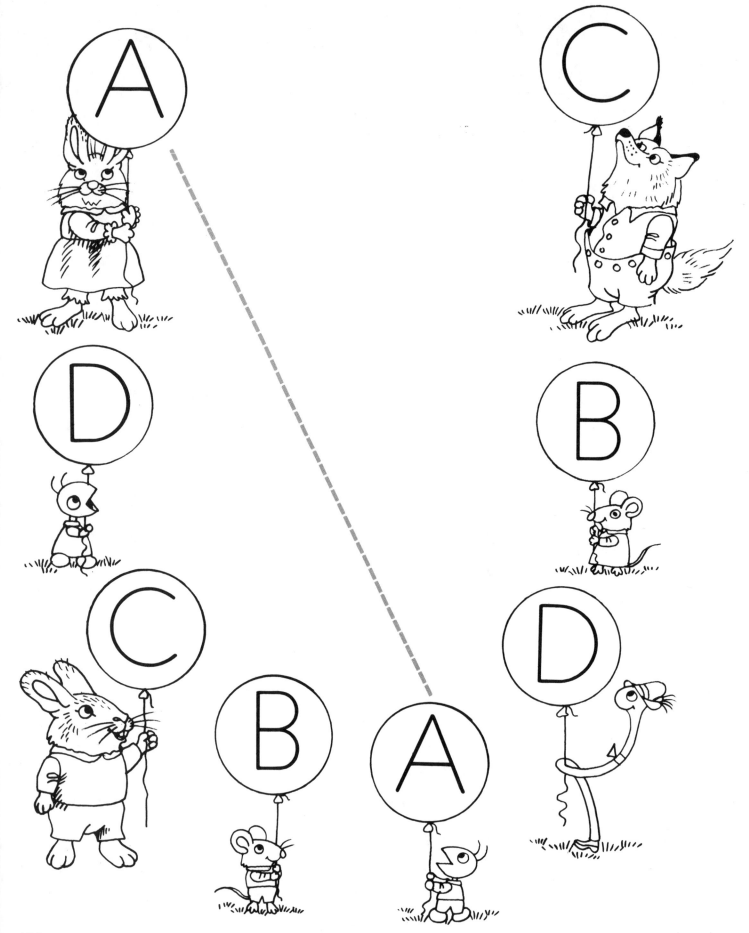